Retold by

Illustrated by

English language consultant: Peter Viney

Contents

You can listen to the story online here:
www.usborneenglishreaders.com/
princessandthepea

This is Prince Florian.
Prince Florian has a good life.
He lives in a palace with his father
and mother, the King and Queen.

He has no brothers and sisters.
Sometimes Prince Florian is lonely.
One day, he tells his mother and
father, "I want to get married."

"That's wonderful!" they say.
"When can we meet her?"
"There isn't anyone just now. Can you help me?" says Prince Florian.

I want to marry a princess - a real princess.

"There are lots of real princesses in the world," says his father.

Prince Florian goes to meet
some princesses.

I am a real princess. My family is very old.

Princess Irma

I am a real princess. My family is very rich.

Princess Noor

I am a real princess. Look at me. I'm beautiful.

Princess Hania

Prince Florian listens to them all. They tell him about their palaces, their families and their clothes. They are not interested in Prince Florian.

The prince goes home again.

"What do you think?" asks the Queen.

"I don't know," says Prince Florian. "*Are* they real princesses? I just don't know."

In the night, there is a storm.
It rains and rains.
"There's somebody at the door,"
says a servant.
Prince Florian goes to the door.
A girl is standing there, in the storm.

"Wait," says Prince Florian. "Your
clothes are all wet. Let's find some
dry clothes for you."

"Oh, thank you," says the girl.

"Are you a princess? A *real* princess?"
Florian asks.

"A real princess," the girl says,
and she smiles.

Prince Florian tells his mother. "She's very nice, but *is* she a real princess? How can we know?"

Princess Rosamond comes in. "Thank you for everything," she says. "Are you hungry?" asks Prince Florian. "Let's have some food."

The prince and princess talk and talk. Princess Rosamond asks Prince Florian lots of questions. She is interested in everything.

The King and Queen smile. They like Princess Rosamond. Prince Florian likes her too.

The Queen goes to one of the bedrooms. She tells a servant, "Let's make a bed for Princess Rosamond." She puts a dry green pea on the bed. "We need twenty mattresses," she says, "and twenty quilts."

She takes Princess Rosamond to the bedroom. "Are you tired?" she asks. "You can sleep in this room."

"Thank you," says Princess Rosamond. "I *am* a little tired."

The next morning, Princess
Rosamond comes into the room.

"You look tired again today," says
the Queen.

"I'm sorry," says the princess.
"It's the bed. There's something in it –
a little thing. It hurts my back and I
can't sleep."

"I'm sorry," the princess says again.

"Can you really feel a little pea under twenty mattresses and twenty quilts?" asks the queen. "That's good. It means you're a real princess."

"That's wonderful!" says Prince Florian.

All day, the prince and princess talk. Princess Rosamond tells Florian about her life. She is lonely too.

"Let's get married," says Prince Florian.

"Yes, let's," says Princess Rosamond. "But Florian, can I ask you something? When we are married, please can we have a different bed? With no peas in it?" She smiles, and Florian laughs.

"Yes, we can," he says.

Family words

Family words are important words.
We use them a lot. Do you know these words?

Grandparents

Grandfather   Grandmother

Parents

Father   Mother

Children

Brother   Sister

Pets

Home   Dog   Cat

All families are different. (Prince Florian has no
brothers and sisters.) Who is in your family?

Activities

The answers are on page 24.

Can you see it in the picture?
Which three things *can't* you see?

cat   dog   flower   king

palace   prince   princess   queen

servant   sky   tree   water

Talk about people in the story

Choose the right words.

beautiful	difficult	happy
interested	lonely	sorry

1.

Prince Florian is ....

2.

Princess Hania is ....

3.

Princess Rosamond is
.... in everything.

4.

"I'm ....
I can't sleep."

Princess Rosamond

What is Princess Rosamond thinking?
Choose the right words.

Please, tell me all about it.

He's nice!

I'm really happy!

I'm all cold and wet.

1.

2.

3.

4.

Which princess?

Choose *two* things to say about each princess.

Princess Irma

Princess Noor

Princess Hania

A. She is wearing a red dress.

B. She is wearing a hat.

C. She is holding a small dog.

D. She is holding a picture.

E. She has a car.

F. She is in a big room.

What are they saying?

There are some wrong words here.
Can you choose the right word?

find   hear   meet

black   dry   special

funny   hungry   tired

Word list

interested (adj) when you are interested, you want to know all about something.

life (n) your life can be the time that you live (how many years), or the way that you live.

lonely (adj) when you are alone and you don't want to be, you are lonely.

mattress (v) a mattress is like a large, soft cushion on a bed. You sleep on a mattress.

palace (n) the home of a king or queen.

pea (n) a small round green vegetable.

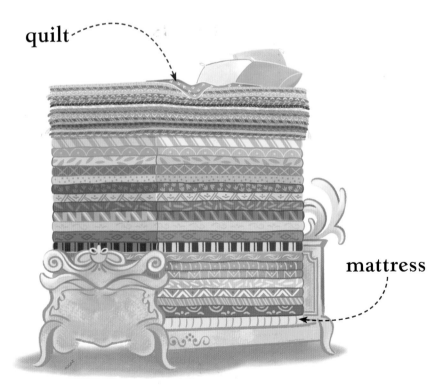

quilt

mattress

prince (n) the son of a king or queen. The daughter of a king or queen is a **princess**.

quilt (n) a quilt is like a large, thin cushion on a bed. It covers your body and you sleep under it.

servant (n) a person who works for another person in their home.

storm (n) a kind of very bad weather. A storm can have a lot of rain, snow or wind, and sometimes thunder and lightning.

wonderful (adj) when something is wonderful, it is really good.

servants

Answers

Can you see it in the picture?

Three things you can't see:
cat, princess, servant.

Talk about people in the story

1. lonely
2. beautiful
3. interested
4. sorry

Princess Rosamond

1. I'm all cold and wet.
2. He's nice!
3. Please, tell me all about it.
4. I'm really happy!

Which princess?

Princess Irma - B, D.
Princess Noor - A, E.
Princess Hania - C, F.

What are they saying?

1. ~~ask~~ meet
2. ~~old~~ dry
3. ~~nice~~ tired

You can find information about
other Usborne English Readers here:
www.usborneenglishreaders.com

Designed by Hope Reynolds
Series designer: Laura Nelson Norris
Edited by Jane Chisholm
Digital imaging: John Russell

First published in 2019 by Usborne Publishing Ltd.,
Usborne House, 83-85 Saffron Hill, London EC1N 8RT, England.
www.usborne.com Copyright © 2019 Usborne Publishing Ltd.